The INTERGALACTIC PETTING ZOO

AND OTHER STORIES

Teeny Weenies

The
INTERGALACTIC
PETTING ZOO

AND OTHER STORIES

DAVID LUBAR

ILLUSTRATED BY BILL MAYER

STARSCAPE

A TOM DOHERTY ASSOCIATES BOOK

NEW YORK

THE INTERGALACTIC PETTING ZOO AND OTHER STORIES

Copyright © 2019 by David Lubar

Illustrations copyright © 2019 by Bill Mayer

A Starscape Book
Published by Tom Doherty Associates
175 Fifth Avenue
New York, NY 10010

www.tor-forge.com

Library of Congress Cataloging-in-Publication Data

Names: Lubar, David, author. | Mayer, Bill (Illustrator), illustrator.
Title: Teeny weenies tales : the Intergalactic Petting Zoo and other stories / David Lubar ; illustrated by Bill Mayer.
Description: First edition. | New York : Tom Doherty Associates, 2019. | "A Starscape Book." | Summary: A selection of twelve stories about aliens, a community pool filled with bullies, a surprising start to the Fourth of July fireworks, and other peculiar things, with comic-book style illustrations.
Identifiers: LCCN 2018048321| ISBN 9781250173423 (hardcover : alk. paper) | ISBN 9781250187710 (ebook)
Subjects: LCSH: Paranormal fiction. | Children's stories, American. | CYAC: Supernatural—Fiction. | Short stories.
Classification: LCC PZ7.L96775 Tem 2019 | DDC [Fic]—dc23
LC record available at https://lccn.loc.gov/2018048321

Our books may be purchased in bulk for promotional, educational, or business use. Please contact your local bookseller or the Macmillan Corporate and Premium Sales Department at 1-800-221-7945, extension 5442, or by email at MacmillanSpecialMarkets@macmillan.com.

First Edition: April 2019

Printed in the United States of America

0 9 8 7 6 5 4 3 2 1

For Leslie Blatt, who brought me there;
Susan Teitelbaum, who wrangled the writers;
Pam Gunter, Wayne Rush, Bruce DuBoff, and
the rest of the wonderful members of the New Jersey
Association of School Librarians.

Thank you for always making me feel like
I'm coming home.

CONTENTS

THE
INTERGALACTIC
PETTING ZOO

would love to explore outer space, or the deepest parts of the ocean. But whenever my dad said, "Let's explore!" all that meant was we were going to drive somewhere we hadn't been before, looking for something to do. We would all bundle into the car—Mom, Dad, me, and my little brother and sister, Lenni and Azelia, and go off in search of fun.

Dad especially liked roadside attractions. Sometimes, that worked out okay. We've been to a cave about an hour and a half west of here, and to a big model-railroad display just five miles south. And there's a nice car museum in town.

But we've also been to a plumbing museum, which is just about as exciting as it sounds. Imagine ten rooms filled with faucets, pipes, sinks, drains, plungers, bathtubs, and toilets. And we spent the longest two hours of my life at a natural-fiber museum. Yeah, I got to see endless types of yarn, miles of thread, and a glass tank full of hardworking silkworms.

Today, something caught my eye as Dad took a random exit off Route 80 and headed north.

There was a billboard that had an ad for *Zorg's Intergalactic Petting Zoo.* I didn't say anything. I figured, with a name like that, it would be a big disappointment. I could picture some goats with fake pairs of extra eyes glued on their foreheads, or pigs painted with purple stripes.

Unfortunately, the ad caught Dad's eye, too.

"Look, kids!" he said. "I think we've found our next destination. This will be amazing!"

I wasn't surprised by his enthusiasm. A hand-lettered sign on a piece of cardboard, nailed to a telephone pole, can catch his interest. A poorly painted sheet of plywood leaning against a rock on the ground can get him excited. But an actual professionally printed billboard towering over the roadside turns him into a total family-trip Weenie. Mom calls them *tourist traps,* but she's just as big a fan of roadside attractions as Dad is.

We followed the directions on the billboard, and ended up bouncing along a small dirt road that led us to the entrance for Zorg's Intergalactic Petting Zoo.

The building was shaped like a giant flying saucer. It was actually better built than I'd expected. A lot of these places were slapped together with plywood, and looked like they'd fall apart when the wind picked up. This one was made of metal, and looked like it was designed by someone who actually understood spaceflight. But I still didn't get my hopes up.

We parked in the lot, then headed for the saucer, where an entrance sign with an arrow pointed to a section outlined in green lights.

A ramp came down.

We walked up.

There was a guy dressed in silver coveralls standing behind a ticket counter. He was shaped like a human, but with an enormous head. A single ear wrapped from one side of his head to the other. His nose had a pair of slits shaped like the holes in a violin. Instead of hair, he had purple scales. I hated to think what it felt like to wear that mask all day.

"Welcome. I am Zorg," he said, in a fake alien voice.

"Five tickets, please," Mom said. "Two adult, three children."

We got our tickets and headed down a corridor, into the first room.

"Lambs!" Azelia squealed. She ran over to a pen that held three costumed wooly creatures behind a low fence. They were dyed blue, and had a second set of ears. The sign on the wall behind them read: *Wooly Niknaks from Aldebus VII.*

I figured that would be the seventh planet orbiting a star named Aldebus. I also figured there was no point being a grump, so I went along with things and petted the *alien* lambs. The wool felt weird, like spaghetti. Obviously, "Zorg" had sprayed something on the sheep.

"They're so cute!" Lenni said.

Azelia wrapped her arms around a lamb. "I want to take you home!"

"They certainly are adorable," Mom said.

"But they're staying right here," Dad added, before my sister could get her hopes up. He bought some "Niknak feed" from a vending machine. It looked like dried corn.

After Lenni and Azelia fed the wooly critters, we moved around the room, petting the Rigelian Squealer, which looked like a tattooed pig, the Rare Voldar IX Moo Beast, which was a calf wearing antlers, and other faked-up barnyard animals. They all felt just a bit strange.

Then, we headed down a corridor that led to a room with sea creatures. Some of them, in shallow tanks on the floor, could be petted. I expected them to be slimy, but most of them felt like flannel, or the rug in our living room.

There was a door at the other side of that room. A sign on it promised, *Sol III hominids*.

I'm still kicking myself for reading it without really noticing what it meant.

Anyhow, we opened the door and stepped into a room that looked pretty much like a typical kitchen.

"Sol III," I said as the door clicked shut behind us.

Everyone looked at me. "That's Earth," I said. "And *hominids*—I think that means us."

The floor lurched, like the whole building had jumped.

Dad grabbed the door and yanked at it.

"Locked," he said.

"How cute!"

"Adorable!"

"I want to take one home!"

I followed the voices toward the ceiling. There was a large opening near the top of the wall. A creature that looked like an elephant with trunks for arms towered over me. I couldn't tell for sure from below, but it was probably about ten or twelve feet tall. Two smaller versions, at seven or eight feet, stood in front of it. I guess those were the kids.

One of the kids reached down and rubbed my back with a rubbery trunk.

I was about to scream, but it actually felt kind of nice. The tip of the trunk reminded me of the scrub brush my folks keep in the shower.

Another of the kids reached into a sack and pulled out a cheeseburger. It waved it in the air, over my head. I leaped, but couldn't quite reach it.

The parent creature tapped the kid on the shoulder, then pointed to me, as if telling the kid to stop teasing me. The kid dropped the burger into my hands.

It was pretty good.

So here we are, the Sol III hominids in Zorg's Intergalactic Petting Zoo. It looked like Zorg wasn't wearing a mask, after all. And the Wooly Niknak really wasn't a sheep. I guess it was just our luck that, out of all the fake roadside attractions and tourist traps, we had to stumble into the real thing. And to become a part of it.

Come see us sometime, if you get the chance. And don't forget I like having my back scratched.

ROOT, ROOT, ROOT FOR THE HOME TEAM

Bentley was perfectly happy sitting on the living room floor in his pajamas, watching cartoons. But he knew his morning was about to get ruined.

"Come on, Bentley, get dressed," his dad said. "Your sister has a game."

"I don't care," Bentley said. "I want to stay here."

"You'll turn into a couch potato," his dad said.

"I'm on the floor," Bentley said.

"Then you'll be a floor potato," his dad said.

"That's fine with me," Bentley said. "I like potatoes."

He begged and pleaded, but it was a losing battle, just like it always was. His parents insisted on dragging him out to his sister's softball games every weekend. That wasn't fair. Bentley had to sit in the stands and watch softball, when he could have stayed home and watched something interesting.

Well, if he couldn't stay home, he could at least sit where he wanted.

When Bentley and his family got to the field, his sister went to join her team on the home-team bench. His parents went to the bleachers.

"What a bunch of bleacher Weenies," Bentley muttered as he walked away from them and plunked down on the ground behind the fence that ran along the first-base line.

"Bentley," his mom called. "Come sit with us. You'll miss the game."

"I can see it fine from here," he shouted back.

Bentley expected her to argue, but she didn't say anything more. He settled into his spot and waited for the game to begin. He was eager for it to start because the sooner it started, the sooner it would end. And then, at least, they could go for ice cream.

"Don't forget to root," his dad called.

"I won't," Bentley said.

When his sister hit a double, Bentley could hear his parents shouting, "Yay!" and "Way to go, Shana!"

Bentley waved his hands in the air and, in a voice dripping with boredom said, "Root, root, root." That almost made him happy, because it really looked like he was rooting. He figured that would stop his parents from bothering him.

"I wish I'd thought of this sooner," Bentley said to himself.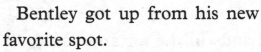

Every time his sister's team scored, he waved his arms wildly and shouted "Root, root, root."

It was the most fun he'd ever had at a softball game.

Finally, the game ended. It was time for ice cream. And then, after a double scoop of chocolate-brownie chunk or peanut-butter fudge ripple, he could go back home and watch more cartoons.

"Let's get moving, Bentley," his dad said, walking up to him from behind.

Bentley got up from his new favorite spot.

Or, at least he tried to.

"Come on, hurry up," Shana said. "Everyone is waiting."

"I'm trying." Bentley pushed against the ground with his hands and feet. But he couldn't get up. He felt as if his rear end had been glued to the earth.

His dad squatted next to him. "Oh, no . . ." he said.

"What?" Bentley asked.

"It looks like you grew roots," his dad said.

"What!" Bentley felt under his butt on either side, with both hands.

Or he tried to. Something blocked his fingers.

"Those are definitely roots," his mom said as she knelt on the other side of Bentley.

"Looks like you really rooted for me," Shana said.

Bentley pushed harder. It was no use. He was firmly rooted to the ground.

"I guess we could try to dig him up," his dad said.

"Can we get ice cream first?" Shana asked.

"Of course," Bentley's mom said. "He's not going anywhere."

"Or we could leave him here until the

season is over," Shana said. "That way, he won't miss any games."

"That's not a bad idea," Bentley's dad said.

"It might be safer," his mom said. "The roots are there for a reason. Come on. Let's go before the line gets too long."

"Hey, no, wait!" Bentley shouted as everyone walked off.

They kept going.

Bentley hoped they'd come back soon. And he hoped they'd bring him ice cream. And a shovel. As much as he liked being a couch potato, or a floor potato, being a field potato was no fun at all.

THE BULLY POOL

Gramps was visiting us for the summer. He'd grown up here in Flatsbern Hills, New Jersey, but he moved to Denver three years ago to teach art at the University of Colorado. I'd been begging him all week to take a walk to the town park. Today, we finally did.

"Is that where it happened?" I asked when we reached the fence that ran around the community pool. Kids were swimming and splashing and having a ball.

"That's the place," he said. "But it looks a lot different. They had to rebuild the pool. It was pretty much destroyed."

"And you were there?" I asked.

He smiled. "I sure was. It's a day I'll never forget."

I'd heard stories in school about the big disaster at the town pool, but none of my friends knew for sure what had happened. Everyone had a different version.

Gramps walked over to one of the picnic tables next to the pool. "Have a seat, Tristan. I'll tell you all about it."

I plopped down on the bench and sprawled out. I didn't need to save room for Gramps. He paced when he talked. He has a lot of energy. He almost never sits.

"It was a hot July day, a lot like this one," he said. "I was seven. We were all at the pool, because it was Founder's Day. It was a great celebration for the whole town. The school band played. We had footraces and a pie-eating contest. There were huge platters of food spread out for everyone to enjoy. A lot of us brought sparklers to light when it got dark."

"I've never heard of Founder's Day," I said.

"They don't do it anymore," Gramps said. "Not after what happened."

I waited for him to continue.

"We ate heaping plates full of food," Gramps said. "Back then, a lot of parents believed you'd get bad cramps if you went swimming right after eating. So we had to wait awhile. But later, we went into the pool to cool off. There was this one boy—let's call him Howard— who wasn't a good swimmer."

"I'm a good swimmer," I said. I looked at the lanes in the deep end. I could swim laps for hours without getting tired.

"I know. I made sure your folks taught you when you were real young. Howard wasn't so lucky. When he tried to swim, he looked like a creature that had never seen a pool, or even a puddle. So the lifeguard sent him there." Gramps pointed to the kiddie section, which had been walled off at the shallow end of the pool.

"That must have made him feel bad." I'd hate to have to leave all my friends and wade around by myself.

"I'm sure it did," Gramps said. "And he was there all alone. That's how the trouble started. A kid who's alone and unhappy is a magnet for bullies."

Gramps stopped pacing and stared toward the kiddie pool. A cluster of little kids splashed around in water up to their chests. He seemed to be looking into the past.

After a minute, he went back to the story. "I think Dempsey Starkmonger got the idea first. He was a mean brute. Big and mean on the outside, but like most bullies, he was nothing more than a little Weenie on the inside. Still, we all stayed out of his way. When he spotted Howard, he climbed out of the pool, ran over to the kiddie section, leaped as high as he could, and yelled, 'Cannonball!'

"He splashed down right next to Howard. The wave nearly knocked the kid off his feet."

"And then other bullies did it?" I asked. That's what I'd heard.

"They sure did," Gramps said. "One after another. And not just the bullies in the pool. It was like they were being drawn from all over town. Sort of like when sharks smell blood."

"Poor Howard," I said.

Gramps nodded. "Before he knew it, he was surrounded by bullies. And more kept coming. Each one did a cannonball dive. The water got more and more crowded. Soon, there was almost no room for anyone else to fit. But they still kept coming. They filled the whole kiddie pool solid. Imagine that."

I looked at the pool, and tried to picture a solid mass of bullies.

"The last bully barely managed to cram himself into the last tiny bit of space. There was no splash now. There wasn't any room for it."

Gramps paced between me and the fence. "The kiddie pool was plugged tight with bully flesh, wall to wall."

"And then what?" I asked. We were finally at the part everyone talked about. I couldn't wait to find out the truth.

"They were stuck," Gramps said. "Crammed so tight, none of them could get free. Like olives in an overstuffed jar. The lifeguards tried to pull them out. They couldn't do it. They called the fire department. They couldn't do it, either.

"Finally, the police chief, who wasn't fond of bullies, had an idea. 'Let them starve for a while,' he said. 'Then, there'll be room to move.'"

"How long did that take?" I asked. I couldn't imagine spending a whole day, or more, wedged against a bunch of other kids.

"Nobody knows. As soon as the bullies heard they were going to be starved free, they started wailing and moaning. It had already been three or four hours since they'd eaten. Even if they weren't really hungry yet, the threat of starvation was enough to get their stomachs rumbling. Some of the parents felt sorry for them, even though they'd gotten themselves into this mess. One father ran to the picnic area and grabbed some food for his starving darling. Then a mother snatched up some food for her little brute. Next thing you know, all these parents were racing to the picnic tables and grabbing heaping plates of the only food that was left."

"Baked beans?" I guessed. Whenever I went to a picnic or cookout, the burgers and hot dogs were the first to go. And then, the macaroni salad got scooped up. But there were always lots of beans left. "So they turned into beanie Weenies."

"That's right," Gramps said. "All the parents were feeding their kids baked beans, to stop them from crying."

"Wouldn't that make them get even tighter?" I asked. "So they'd be stuck for longer."

"Yup. It would make things worse. And it

would make them gassy," Gramps said. "You know what they say about beans, right?"

"I sure do," I said. "They're good for your heart."

"And a musical fruit," Gramps added. "After a while, you could hear it." He put the back of his hand against his mouth and made a fart sound.

I couldn't help laughing. It's not the sort of thing you expect a grandfather to do. "That must have stunk," I said.

"Well, it would have, if the gas had anywhere to go." Gramps slowly shook his head, as if even he couldn't believe what he was about to tell me. "But they were wedged so tightly, the gas was trapped. The farts kept coming. It started out as little toots. But after a while, it sounded like the testing room of a tuba factory."

Gramps paused to demonstrate the rising fart volume on the back of his hand. Then he picked up the story where he'd left off.

"The pressure kept building beneath them.

Eventually, something had to give. I think it was Dempsey who made that final monster fart, just when it was starting to get dark. They all shot out of the pool like corks out of a bottle."

"Wow . . ." I said. "That must have been an amazing thing to see."

"It was definitely unforgettable. And that would have been the end of it, if someone hadn't picked the exact same moment to light a sparkler and wave it around near the pool."

Gramps waved his hand like he was holding one.

"What's wrong with that?" I asked.

"Farts contain methane gas," he said. "And methane is very flammable. One little spark can set it off. I think there's some hydrogen in a fart, too. Which doesn't help. All that gas got lit. Kaboom! It made one fierce and fiery explosion. It flung all the bullies high in the air and burned their butts like they'd squatted over a blowtorch. Some of them couldn't sit down for weeks."

Gramps stopped pacing. I guess that was the end of the story.

"Was Howard okay?" I asked.

"He was smaller than the bullies, so he shot up higher," Gramps said. "His bottom hardly got warmed by the blast."

"That seems fair," I said. "What happened to the bullies?"

"The same thing that always happens whenever a group of kids misbehave. Some of them got punished by their parents. Some of them got treated like they were innocent victims. Some of them grew up to be bullies. Some of them grew up to be better people." Gramps nodded in the direction of our home. "We should be heading back."

I got off the bench. There was one more thing I had to know. The way Gramps told the story, it wasn't just like he'd been there watching what happened. It was like he'd actually been part of it. I thought about how much sympathy he had for the victim. "The kid you called Howard. Was that you?"

"No. I wasn't Howard," Gramps said.

"But you were there, right?" I asked.

"Definitely." Gramps laughed. "You could say I was stuck right in the middle of things."

I thought about how he never liked to sit for long. I guess Gramps was one of the bullies who'd gotten his butt toasted.

That made me feel terrible. I didn't like the idea of Gramps being mean to people. And I sure didn't want to be the grandson of a bully.

Then, I remembered he'd also talked about how people could change. I realized this made the whole story all that more wonderful and amazing, and that made me feel happy again. He'd gotten his butt burned, but it had turned him into a better person.

So now I know the real story about what happened at the town pool all those years ago. And I'm pretty sure I also know why, when Gramps is here for dinner, he never eats his beans.

VISIBILITY

My uncle Ralph and my aunt Lucy are mad scientists. Seriously. They're always coming up with weird inventions. Whenever I ask them why, they laugh and say, "We want to take over the world for the good of humanity!"

So far, the world has been pretty safe from them. Though they did manage to blow a hole in the side of their house once. Or maybe it was twice.

I stay with them for two weeks each summer, while my parents go on a trip by themselves. It doesn't bother me that my parents go without me, because they usually end up somewhere boring. Uncle Ralph and Aunt Lucy, on the other hand, are never boring. They love science so much, it's not enough to call them nerds. They're total science Weenies, in the best possible way.

They seemed more excited than usual when my parents dropped me off this morning.

"Steffie!" Uncle Ralph cried. "We've been eager to see you."

"But we hope we won't see you for long," Aunt Lucy said. Then she laughed.

I didn't even bother asking what they meant about not seeing me for long. They like to talk like that. It's sort of a code. They told me they always have to be careful that other scientists don't steal their inventions.

I didn't ask them to explain what they did next, either.

Uncle Ralph pulled a tape measure from his pants pocket and checked my height. "No growth spurt yet," he said. "That's good."

Aunt Lucy asked me to step on a scale. She seemed happy with the results.

I figured I'd find out what was going on eventually. As much as they like to be mysterious and throw winks at each other like they are playing catch, they like talking about their discoveries even more. After breakfast, they explained everything.

"We've created our finest invention of all time," Aunt Lucy said.

"You won't believe it," Uncle Ralph said.

"I'm sure I won't," I said.

They were very good at ignoring my sarcasm. I was used to that. Adults ignore kids pretty much all the time, unless we're doing something we don't want them to see.

"We've invented an invisibility ray," Aunt Lucy said.

"That's pretty cool," I said. It actually sounded like a useful invention. "Can I see it?"

As soon as I said those words, I realized I'd made a pretty good joke. I pictured it in a movie, with a scientist talking to his friend.

I invented invisibility.

I can't see how that would work.

"We haven't tried it yet," Uncle Ralph said.

"We needed a subject of the right size and weight," Aunt Lucy said.

"And that would be me?" I asked. Everything they'd been saying and doing suddenly made sense.

"You're the perfect size," my uncle said.

"Are you sure it's safe?' I asked.

"Absolutely," Aunt Lucy said. "We would never risk hurting our favorite niece."

They explained all about it in a way I didn't come close to following. Not that it mattered. I knew I wanted to do it. My mind was already bursting with ideas about all the fun I could have once nobody could see me.

The ray machine didn't have any sort of

cool mad-science look to it. It seemed pretty much like a desk lamp with a lot of extra wires and a pair of weird-shaped bulbs.

When they zapped me, I felt warm, in a pleasant way, like the hot sun was shining right on my face. After they switched off the lamp, I held up my hands. I could see them. I looked over at my aunt and uncle. They stared  at me. Then they sighed. I guess they could see me, too.

"It needs more work," Uncle Ralph said.

Aunt Lucy agreed. They started to discuss what they had to do. I went for a walk. Their house was only a block from town. As I strolled along the sidewalk, a guy came toward me, walking a pair of shelties. Both the guy and the dogs stopped to stare at me as I passed.

That was weird. As a horrible thought hit me, I looked down to make sure my clothes hadn't turned invisible. Luckily, they hadn't.

It got weirder. Everyone stared at me. People walking by, people biking by, and people driving by all watched me. It almost seemed like they couldn't resist watching every move I made. As far as I knew, people passing overhead in airplanes were peering down, though I had no way to test that.

That's when it hit me. I knew what was going on! I raced back home to tell my aunt and uncle the good news. I found them sitting in the kitchen, looking like someone had zapped them with a sadness ray.

"We failed again," Uncle Ralph said.

"This is worse than when we blew the hole in the wall," Aunt Lucy said.

"Worse than both those times," Uncle Ralph said.

They turned their heads as I walked in, and stared at me, as I knew they would.

"You didn't fail," I said.

"We can see you," Uncle Ralph said.

Aunt Lucy nodded. "And you are supposed to be invisible. Therefore, we failed."

"Try not to watch me," I said.

I walked across the kitchen to the refrigerator, then returned to the doorway where I'd come in. Their eyes stayed locked on me the whole time.

"You didn't invent invisibility," I said. "You invented visibility!"

Aunt Lucy leaped from her chair like she'd been jolted by electricity. "She's right!"

"Now, all we have to do is reverse it!" Uncle Ralph said. He raced toward the garage, where they had their lab. "Let's get to work."

"See you later," Aunt Lucy said as she dashed out to join him.

That was a pretty good joke, too. I was glad they had another chance to make their invention work. But I hoped my visibility would wear off sooner or later. It's nice being noticed, once in a while. Just not all the time.

If you see what I mean.

COLLECT
THEM ALL!

The super-duper awesome video game "Xabulose Zeplons" hit the shelves at the perfect time. Summer had just begun. School was out. The days were free.

Every kid on the block in Joey's neighborhood begged for, and got, a copy of the game.

But that was just the start. To enjoy all the secrets of the game, you needed one of the twelve Xabulose Zeplon action figures. But you couldn't just buy them. You had to win the right to do that by playing the game online with your friends.

Adding to the pressure, every group could only have a single copy of each action figure. Adding even more to the pressure, there were eighteen kids in Joey's group. The thought of being one of the half dozen who'd miss out turned even the most casual player into a competitive gamer Weenie. It turned Joey, who was already too competitive, in even darker directions.

Joey's friend Barnaby was the first to discover one of the hidden battle arenas and score a victory there. He earned the secret code to order Sharmatch the Destroyer, a fearsome warrior who carried a huge photon cannon.

"Oh, man," Joey said when he went over to Barnaby's house to see Sharmatch. The figure was a full foot tall, with glowing eyes and a jet pack.

"Check this out," Barnaby said. He launched the game, and there was Sharmatch on the screen, ready to destroy the enemy with his photon cannon as he flew above them.

"Cool . . ." Joey said.

His friend Cassandra was next. She got Endroza, Death Dancer. Then Stuart, down at the house on the corner, got Endroza's twin brother, Endrazo, Life Spinner.

Joey got nothing. He wasn't as good as his friends at games.

Summer crept forward. Time was growing short. All his friends had an action figure. There was only one secret battle arena left. Joey was afraid someone else would get it. And then, he'd have nothing. He went online to look for hints. He found plenty of them. He also found ways to cheat.

Joey hated cheaters. They ruined everything.

But he hated being left out even more.

Joey cheated.

"I'll bet they all cheated," he said as he discovered the last secret arena.

And finally, he won Fath the Finisher, the final Xabulose Zeplon. His parents took the code and ordered the figure. Joey waited in agony, watching for the delivery truck.

Finally, Fath arrived.

"Whoa . . ." Joey said as he unpacked his action figure. Fath wore armor that made him look like a combination of a samurai and a dinosaur. Joey ran to his room, turned on his console, and started the game.

Fath's eyes glowed. Then, he smiled an evil smile.

Joey froze. None of the other figures had smiled.

Fath raised his right arm in victory.

None of the other figures had raised an arm in victory.

Fath raised his left hand, in which he held an atomic disruptor. He fired a beam at Joey, disrupting all of Joey's atoms. Joey was no more.

At his friends' houses, all the other figures raised their arms, and their weapons. Now that Fath had arrived, they were complete. The preparation was finished.

The plan had succeeded.

The invasion could begin.

THE LEFT HAND
OF DORKINESS

You should never call anyone a witch. I guess you should really never call anyone any sort of name. But you should especially never call anyone a witch when that's what they happen to be. I learned that lesson, and one other, at the end of the last day of school.

"Summer vacation!" I said to my friend Krista as the bell rang. "I've been waiting all year for this!"

"Me, too! Summer, here we come," Krista said. "Let's get out of here, Destiny."

"Wait," I said as we left the classroom. "I think I left my sweater in the cafeteria."

"You won't need it," she said. "It's *summer*."

"But I want it," I said.

We headed to the cafeteria. And there she was—the dreaded lunch lady who sat behind the cash register and scowled at everyone. As I snatched my sweater from the chair where I'd left it, I muttered, "I'm glad I won't be seeing you all summer, you witch."

I thought I'd kept my voice down. But she turned her head toward me.

I felt like I'd just swallowed an ice cube. All my insides froze as she stared at me. The worst part was that, for the first time ever, she wasn't scowling. Instead, she smiled at me. And then, in a voice no louder than my own, she said, "You won't see summer at all, dearie."

I stared back, unable to speak.

"Get lost," she whispered. Right after that,

I swear, she cackled like a witch, and ran from the cafeteria.

"What was that about?" I asked Krista. "How could she keep us from seeing summer?"

"No idea. But let's get out of here," she said.

We went to the door on the far side of the cafeteria that led to the parking lot. I pushed the bar. It wouldn't move.

"Locked," I said.

"No problem," Krista said. "We'll just go out the front exit."

"Problem," I said a moment later, when we reached the end of the corridor. It was supposed to turn left. But it turned right. "The hallway is different."

"This is wrong," Krista said. "What should we do?"

"We have to go that way," I said. "There's no other choice."

We turned right. But nothing looked normal or familiar. All the walls were blank, with no posters or lockers. We walked, and took random turns, but we couldn't find a way out.

"I think we've been here before," Krista said as we reached a corridor that made two sharp turns in a row.

"You're right," I said. We turned another corner and found ourselves back at the cafeteria. "It's like a maze."

"I'm terrible at mazes," Krista said. "I can't even solve the easy ones on the kiddie menus at the diner."

"Me, either." I tried to think of a way out. Nothing came to mind except to keep looking. After a while, we passed the gym. Then we passed the cafeteria again. After that, we passed the library.

The lights were still on.

"I think there's someone inside," Krista said.

She was right. Dorky little Noah Gretch sat at a table, hunched over a book. I was about to say, "It's just a silly little reader Weenie." But I'd already learned one lesson today about calling people names. Maybe Noah was also more than a label.

"Hey," I called. "What are you doing here?"

He jerked his head up like he'd been yanked from a dream. Then he looked over at us and frowned. "What am I doing here? I think that's obvious. I'm reading. Or, at least, I was reading until I got interrupted. What are you doing here?"

"We're trapped," I said. "The lunch lady, who is actually a witch, turned the school into a maze."

I didn't expect him to believe me, but he just shrugged and said, "I guess you made her angry."

"Maybe a little bit," I said. "But not enough to deserve this."

"We can't get out," Krista said. "Wait—that means you're trapped, too."

"Sorry," I said. "I didn't mean to get any of us trapped." I guess I felt a little bit bad for Noah, getting caught up in this with us.

"Don't be silly," he said. "You aren't trapped. A maze isn't a prison. It has to have an exit. You can get out."

"How?" I asked.

"Easy. Just do a left-hand search." He raised his own left hand, as if it explained everything. "That always works, unless there's a king's chamber. And that's not hard to deal with, either. I suspect this maze is probably trivial. So the left-hand search is the smart place to start."

Krista and I stared at him. We had no idea what he was talking about.

He sighed and got up. "Okay, I'll show you. Follow me."

"Thank you," I said.

"Yeah, thanks. That's really nice of you," Krista said.

Noah walked into the hall. Then, he put his left hand on the wall next to him. "If we just keep walking, and always keep a hand on the wall to our left, we'll get out after walking around the entire part of the maze between us and the exit."

"That doesn't sound right," I said.

"Do you want to go back to wandering?" Noah asked.

"No. We'll try your way," Krista said. "I think it makes sense."

"Good answer," Noah said. "Oh, and by the way, most people call it a right-hand search. But I'm a lefty." He tapped the wall, as if to emphasize this, and headed down the hallway.

So we followed him. We walked pretty far. But I'm pretty sure we didn't come back to the same spot over and over, like we'd done before. Anytime we passed a spot I recognized, we were going in the opposite direction from when we first passed it. I was actually starting to understand what we were doing.

"There's the exit!" Krista shouted as we turned a corner and found ourselves facing the front door.

"It worked!" I said.

"Of course it worked." Noah shrugged, as if

saving us from wandering around the school all summer was no big deal. Then, he turned away.

"Where are you going?" I asked.

"Back to the library," he said.

"But school's out. Summer is here," I said. "The place will be empty."

Noah glanced back over his shoulder at us and smiled.

"I know," he said. "I've been waiting all year for this."

Then he put his right hand on the wall, and walked off.

RIDE 'EM, TENDERFOOT!

I see my cousins Bobby and Irene twice a year. They come out to San Jose in the winter, and my family and I go out to Montana in the summer. They live about an hour away from Billings. We usually have a good time together. But they were really distracted this year. There was a new junior rodeo coming to town right toward the end of my visit, and they were both practicing real hard for the events they planned to enter.

Irene was going to do calf roping and barrel riding. Bobby was signed up for calf roping and bull riding.

"I want to do that," I said when they told me about the events. "Bull riding looks like fun."

"Forget it," Bobby said. "You'll get killed. It's not as easy as it looks. I've been training for months."

"How hard can it be?" I asked. I turned toward my parents. "Can I do it?"

"It does sound dangerous," my mom said.

"I do BMX," I said. "I ride down mountains. Dad took me rock climbing last fall."

Mom and Dad exchanged looks. I could tell I was going to get what I wanted. They aren't super-protective, like some of my friends' parents. Dad and I love roller coasters, and Mom and I went for a balloon ride last year for my birthday.

So I had permission from them. And I was  really eager to show Bobby that a city kid from the left coast, as he called California, could do just as well as a cowboy. Or cowkid, or whatever he was.

My cousins didn't have a bull to practice with, so they used a calf. I followed them out to the barn when they were ready for a session. The calf wasn't super-interested in throwing anybody off. But at least that gave Bobby a chance to show me the basics.

Of course, the whole time he was telling me about the right way to sit, and all that stuff, he kept adding, "You're going to get slaughtered. The top of a bull is no place for a cowboy-wannabe tenderfoot Weenie."

I wasn't worried.

At least, I wasn't worried before the rodeo started. And I was fine for the first batch of events. It was exciting watching my cousins rope calves and ride around a row of barrels as fast as they could. Irene took second place in both her events, and Bobby took third in roping.

And then, I got my first look at the bulls we'd be riding.

Bobby, who was sitting next to me in the stands, must have felt my body jolt when I saw the beasts.

"Not at all like a calf, huh?" he said, grinning.

"It does look kind of big," I said. "Are you sure it's not a dinosaur?" I tried to picture myself sitting on it.

"You can back out. Nobody will make fun of you for that," he said.

"No way," I said.

"I guess you're going to get killed," he said.

"I guess you're going to be surprised." I followed him down to the contestant area. Everyone looked excited and nervous. Except for the bulls. They looked annoyed. This was not a good sign.

I was going to be the last rider. That was nice. It would give me a chance to watch everyone else, and maybe even learn a thing or two, besides what Bobby had taught me.

I didn't learn much from the first rider.

He lasted about half a second. The bull twisted and bucked, and the kid went flying through the air. I flinched as he hit the ground. Two guys dressed like clowns distracted the bull so the kid could crawl to safety. He was limping, but he didn't look like he'd taken any permanent damage.

"That didn't seem so bad," I said. "I fall harder than that all the time."

Bobby just snorted. He sounded sort of like a bull. But a small one.

The next two kids did a bit better, and then another one got tossed immediately.

"Maybe you can beat his record for shortest ride," Bobby said.

"Do they give a prize for that?" I asked.

'Nope." He shook his head. Then, he said, "I'm up next. Wish me luck."

"Good luck," I said. I meant it. I wanted him to do well. The better he did, the more I'd enjoy beating his score. Though I still didn't really understand how the scoring worked.

Not that it mattered. I was going to stay on the bull until it gave up and accepted me as its rider.

Bobby took his seat. They opened the gate, letting the bull out. It bucked hard, and he almost flew off, but he held on.

"Go, Bobby!" I screamed as he survived a series of twists, turns, jolts, and bucks. Finally, a rider came over and scooped him off the bull. I guess he'd gone as far as he had to.

After two more kids got flung through the air like pancakes flipped off a hot griddle, it was my turn.

The bull was definitely not a calf.

The instant I got on, I realized I'd made a huge mistake. I felt like I was sitting on the world's largest coiled steel spring.

"Stop!" I screamed just as the gate opened.

At that point, *stop* stopped being an option. Seven thousand pounds of muscle set its mind to throwing me off.

Somehow, I hung on. Fear is a great way to inspire people to cling to things.

And then, the bull did something it hadn't done before. It thrust its head down so far its nose almost touched the ground and kicked up its hind legs. I slid right off, headfirst. I tucked my head, rolled, and landed on my back, right at the bull's front hooves, staring up at his snout. I leaped to my feet. I knew I had to get away.

Before I could escape, the bull leaped on top of me.

Yeah, I know it's hard to picture, but that's what he did. He landed right on my shoulders. If this surprises you, think how I felt. Something gave me the strength to take a step. And then, I took another. And then, I got angry, which gave me even more strength.

I twisted. I bucked. I jolted and spun. I was afraid he'd stay on forever. Finally, with two sudden twists and a sharp shrug of my shoulders, I threw the bull off and staggered out of the arena.

Nobody in the crowd seemed surprised. I guess there's a lot about rodeo I still didn't know.

Bobby got a first-place trophy. I didn't get anything. But the bull did. He got second place for his ride.

I think I'm done with bull riding.

BOOM!

My friends and I always get together to watch the fireworks on the Fourth of July. We used to have to go downtown to the football stadium at the high school. But they switched things up this year, and were shooting them off right across the river, on an old concrete dock, so we'd get a good view from the park that's down the road from my house.

There's a small outdoor stage right by the riverbank, with plenty of seats facing the water. That would be a perfect spot to enjoy the show. It was just starting to get dark when we set out, so we knew we wouldn't have to wait much longer.

"I wish we had some fireworks," my friend Dwight said.

"Me, too. It would be great to have anything," I said. Fireworks weren't legal here. My cousin lives down South. Whenever I visit him he has these awesome rockets, and all sorts of stuff.

"Even a couple small firecrackers would be nice," Dwight said.

That's when Candace tapped me on the shoulder and said, "Guess what?" She's my neighbor, and a friend. She's also a fireworks Weenie. She'll go anywhere there's a display, or even a couple skyrockets or Roman candles, like they shoot off on Friday nights at the local minor league baseball games.

"What?" I asked.

"I found this in the back of a closet at my uncle's house." She held up something that looked like a small stick of dynamite.

Just then, a loud boom startled me. I actually felt the ground shake a little. I looked at the flash of light in the sky above the river. They'd shot up a test rocket. I knew about that. They test three or four of the fireworks before the show, to make sure things run smoothly. Everyone except my neighbor Toby jumped. I guess he didn't even hear the boom.

I looked back at Candace and pointed to the thing in her hand. "What is that? It's huge."

"Quarter stick," Dwight said.

"No way," Candace said. "Those are a lot smaller."

"What do you think, Toby?" I asked.

He was standing there, bobbing his head in time with his music. He always had headphones on. They played music and also cancelled noise. It was a pain trying to get his attention. But he knew all kinds of things, and I figured he'd have a good idea about fireworks. I reached out and lifted one of the headphones. Once I knew I had his attention, I repeated my question.

"That's a half stick," he said. "It makes a big bang. Be careful. It will take your hand right off, and the rest of your arm, too."

Fear and excitement wrestled in my gut. Fear lost.

"We have to do it," I said.

The others nodded.

"Where?" Dwight asked. "We'll get in trouble if we blow anything up."

"The cave!" Candace said.

"Great idea," I said. The cave was really just a place where some boulders had fallen off the side of a cliff and ended up in a pile. There was an open area at the bottom of the pile, big enough for a small kid to sneak into when we played hide-and-seek.

We crossed the park, and reached the cave. As Candace put the half stick down inside the opening, another boom startled me. I watched the flash from the test rocket fade. If I could feel the explosion from so far away,

maybe it was a bad idea for us to light the half stick.

"Step back," Candace said. She pulled a pack of matches from her pocket and knelt down. "We don't want to be close when it goes off."

"Be careful," I said. I realized it was too late to stop her. And I guess I still really wanted to see what would happen. Maybe I was a bit of a fireworks Weenie, too.

The rest of us backed off far enough to reach one of the old oak trees. We stepped behind it for cover. Candace lit the fuse, then ran to join us.

I think we were still too close. The explosion was way louder than I'd expected. Even with the tree between me and the cave, the force of the blast almost knocked me off my feet. The flash dazzled me. Candace and Dwight looked pretty stunned, too. Toby looked fine. He was still bobbing his head to the music. I felt sort of sorry for him because he missed out on so much.

"Wow," I said as the boom from the half stick rang in my ears. "That was—"

I didn't finish my sentence. The ground shook so hard, I staggered, bumping into the tree, and then into Dwight. We grabbed each other to steady ourselves.

But unlike with the fireworks, the shaking didn't stop.

It got worse.

"I think we broke something!" Candace yelled.

She was right. The ground collapsed beneath us. We fell into a pit.

"We started an earthquake!" I said.

I wish I'd been right about that. But as we got back to our feet in the pit, I saw we'd done something far worse.

All of us screamed as the monster we'd awakened burst from the crumbled ground and rose to full height. He looked like a man made of stone and steel. He had the face of

a bat, with huge, pointed ears, and the arms of a body builder. He stomped his foot, and the ground trembled again. I was afraid the earth would open up even wider and swallow us into a bottomless pit.

Another boom shook the sky. I guess they'd fired a third test rocket.

The monster howled in rage and spun toward the firework. Then, he punched a boulder, shattering it.

"It's the sound," Candace said. "He hates it."

The monster turned back toward us. His eyes locked on mine. He staggered toward me.

I searched for any way to escape. The sides of the pit were too steep to climb quickly. I pictured myself getting slammed with a fist that could shatter a boulder. There was no way

I'd survive that. I had to do something to save us.

As the monster closed the distance between us, I reached out and snatched Toby's headphones.

"Hey!" he shouted.

"Sorry." I leaped toward the monster, reached up as high as I could, and slipped the headphones over his ears.

I hoped I'd made the right decision.

He froze. His forehead wrinkled, like he was thinking hard. Then, his head started bobbing to the music. There was another boom in the sky. He didn't even seem to notice. Instead, he turned away and burrowed back under the ground.

"You saved us," Candace said.

"I guess . . ." I was still too dazzled by everything to think clearly. But I suppose she was right. I really did save us.

"My headphones . . ." Toby said.

"Quiet," I said. "We'll get you another pair."
So we went and watched the fireworks. They were great. And I only flinched a little whenever a loud boom shook the air.

TOOTH TROUBLE

Lyle and Debbie argued about everything. They argued about who could run faster. (Lyle was a better sprinter. Debbie was better at long distances. But neither of them was especially fast.) They argued about who was smarter. (The best answer was probably "neither.") They even argued about who was a better arguer. (They were both excellent in that area.)

They were Weenies in so many different ways, it was pointless to even try to classify them. They were also neighbors, and their parents were best friends. Which meant they ended up on vacation together all the time. This gave them all that much more to argue about. Especially now, when they were with their parents at the beach.

"It's windy," Lyle said as he spread out his towel on the sand.

"Not really," Debbie said. "It's just breezy. But it's definitely hot."

"I've felt a lot hotter weather," Lyle said. "This is just warm."

"Look, I see a dolphin," Debbie said.

"No, you don't. That's a log," Lyle said. "But check out at that seagull!"

"It's not a seagull," Debbie said. "It's a tern."

And so it went.

Eventually, Lyle decided to go for a walk. "I'm the world's best shell spotter," he said as he got up from his towel. "I can find all the rarest ones."

"I'm better," Debbie said, springing up to dash ahead of him. "I can discover shells nobody has ever found before."

 They combed the beach with their eyes, finding mostly broken clam-shells, pieces of horseshoe-crab shell, and pebbles. And then, Lyle shouted, "Shark tooth!"

He thrust his hand out, pointing at a spot three feet ahead of him.

"Saw it first!" Debbie shouted as she flung herself through the air, landing on the tooth. She bounced back to her feet, holding the tooth out for Lyle to see.

"That's mine!" he shouted. He rushed at Debbie, hands out, ready to snatch back his treasure.

"Finders keepers," Debbie said. She faked left, then cut right, causing Lyle to totally miss when he tried to grab the tooth.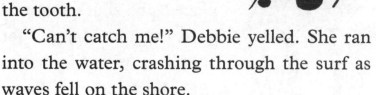

"Can't catch me!" Debbie yelled. She ran into the water, crashing through the surf as waves fell on the shore.

Lyle chased after her.

They ended up waist deep in the warm

water. Lyle kept trying to grab the tooth. Debbie held it high, and leaped away every time he lunged for it.

And then, as she was backing away from Lyle, she slammed into something as firm and broad as the side of a cow.

"Shark!" Lyle screamed, flinging his hand out again, to point at what was, without a doubt, a very large shark, right behind Debbie.

Debbie screamed and jumped away.

The shark rose and opened its gaping jaws, revealing an impossible number of sharp teeth, and one big gap.

"Here, take it back!" Debbie thrust the tooth into the gap. "It's yours. I don't want it."

Once the tooth was replaced, the shark snapped its jaws shut. Happily for Debbie, it waited for her to remove her hand first. Then, it swam off.

"I would have fought it," Lyle said. He started to wade toward shore.

"You would have lost," Debbie said. She followed him into the shallow water. "Ouch," she said as she stepped on something sharp.

"What's that?" Lyle asked.

Debbie reached down and lifted something from the wet sand beneath the foamy surf. "It looks like a shark's tooth, but it's way too big."

"It's not a shark. It's a megalodon," Lyle said. "That's a giant, prehistoric shark."

"Giant . . . prehistoric . . . ?" Debbie asked. She pictured running into something impossibly bigger than the shark she'd just met.

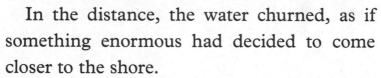

Lyle nodded. "They're supposed to be extinct. But some people think they're still around."

In the distance, the water churned, as if something enormous had decided to come closer to the shore.

"Run!" Debbie screamed as she flung the tooth as far out to sea as she could and made a dash for dry, shark-free land.

For once, Lyle didn't argue.

CAMP MAKAWALLIT

"Guess what, kids?" Mom said.

"What?" my brother, Gavin, and I asked.

"You're going to summer camp!" Mom said.

"Yay!" I shouted. I'd been begging to go to camp ever since last year, when all my friends came back from their camps at the end of the summer and talked about what great times they had.

"Is it Camp Woodside?" That was the one my best friend, Renaldo, went to. It sounded awesome.

Mom shook her head. "No. That's not the one."

"The summer science camp at Trout Lake?" Gavin asked. That was another one we'd heard great things about.

"Nope." Mom shook her head. "It's Camp Makawallit."

I'd never heard of it. And, based on the look on Gavin's face, neither had he.

"I thought you said you couldn't afford camp," Gavin said.

That had been her excuse all year long. She needed to save up for a new dining room table. I felt our table was perfectly fine, except for some scratches and dents Gavin and I had accidently put in it over the past two or three years. But my folks talked all the time about getting a new one. They were total furniture Weenies. We had a blue velvet couch in the living room we weren't even allowed to sit on, and an antique bookcase that was too fragile to hold any books. Mom kept us away from her rolltop desk like it was made of eggshells, and Dad spent way too much time each weekend polishing the cherrywood kitchen cabinets.

"They are very affordable," Mom said. "It's quite a bargain."

I wasn't going to question my good luck.

Maybe I should have.

Mom and Dad dropped us off at the camp a week later. A counselor greeted us. He was wearing a ball cap with "Jimmy" printed on it, and a T-shirt with "Camp Makawallit" in big letters. Under that it read: "A crafty place."

"I hope they mean 'crafty' like spies or silent hunters or something," Gavin said.

"Me, too," I said. It would be fun to sneak around in the woods.

But right after we put our stuff away in our cabin, Jimmy said, "Time's a wasting. Let's get to work."

"Work?" I asked.

"That's just an expression," Jimmy said. "You boys are here to have fun with crafts."

He led us to a large room filled with tables. There were chairs around each table, and kids in almost every chair.

Jimmy grabbed two clear bags from a big bin and handed them to us. Then he pointed to a pair of empty seats. I was happy to see that all the furniture seemed pretty sturdy, and was already scratched up, scuffed, and dented.

My happiness didn't last.

I sat down, then looked at the bag. It had pieces of leather inside. There were thin rectangular pieces, and there were strips. There were also instructions printed on a sheet of paper on the table.

"Looks like we're making a wallet," Gavin said. He sighed and dumped the pieces out in front of him. "Maybe we'll get to go fishing next."

"I didn't see a lake," I said.

"There has to be one," Gavin said. "It's a summer camp. You've seen the ads. They're always filled with watery adventures."

"I hope you're right." I got to work on the wallet. It was actually sort of fun at first, and it was nice imagining giving it to Dad, but I got bored before I was finished.

"Done," I said after I'd made the last stitch. I slapped it down on the table and turned to find Jimmy right behind me.

"Great," he said, picking the wallet up. "You're a quick worker. That's excellent."

Before I could ask what we'd be doing next, he dropped another wallet kit in front of me. I opened my mouth to tell him I was finished with wallets, but he narrowed his eyes and gave me a look that stopped me cold.

So I made another wallet.

And another.

We made wallets all day. I lost count of how many wallets I stitched together.

"If I never see another

99

wallet kit, I'll be happy," Gavin said as we left the building at the end of the day.

"Me, too," I said. My fingers felt like I'd been playing video games for hours with a cheap controller.

We got our wish. The next day, we didn't make wallets. We made baskets. We made more baskets the day after that. Then, we started making key chains. After that, it was back to the wallets. By then, I was pretty sure "Makawallit" was pronounced "make a wallet." It should have been called "Ruinasummer."

Camp lasted for two weeks. They didn't let us call home.

I was so happy to see Mom and Dad when they came for us, I could barely talk. When I finally blurted out how we'd done nothing but make crafts, Mom laughed and said, "You sure do like to exaggerate."

"It's the truth!" Gavin said. "I'll show you." He grabbed Mom's hand and dragged her to the building where we'd made all the wallets, baskets, key chains, and other crafts.

"See?" Gavin cried as he flung the door open.

"See what?" Mom asked.

I stepped up behind them and looked inside. All the bins full of crafts were gone.

Meanwhile, Dad had gone off to talk to Jimmy. I saw Jimmy hand Dad an envelope. By that point, all I wanted to do was go home. But Mom and Dad insisted on stopping at a furniture store on the way back, where they paid for their new dining room 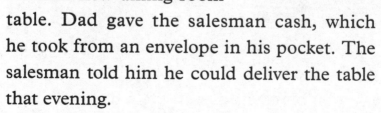 table. Dad gave the salesman cash, which he took from an envelope in his pocket. The salesman told him he could deliver the table that evening.

The next day, when Gavin and I were in town, we saw some of the wallets that we'd made for sale in a store. I read the label: *Makawallit Brand Custom Crafted Wallets.* Below that, it read: *Hand-stitched by highly skilled crafters.* The last line read: *Made in the U.S.A.*

"Come on," I said to Gavin, "we need to get home."

"Why?" he asked.

"We've got a table to ruin," I said.

SUMMER READING (AND SOME AREN'T)

The poster in the library promised: *Summer Reading Is Magic!*

"Yeah, right," Drew said to himself as his mother signed him up for the program.

"You get points for each book you read," the librarian, Mrs. Folger, told him. She turned toward a shelf on the wall behind her. It was lined with toys, games, T-shirts, and other goodies. "You can use the points to win prizes."

That part worked for Drew. He liked prizes. "So how do you know if someone really did the reading?" he asked.

"I trust you," Mrs. Folger said.

That part worked for Drew, too. He checked out three books, and headed home with his mom.

"I wish we could stop for pizza," he said as they were leaving the parking lot.

"If wishes were horses . . ." his mom said. She didn't even bother finishing the expression. She said it so often, Drew knew the rest of it by heart.

If wishes were horses, then beggars would ride.

He figured it meant that if you could wish for what you wanted, anyone could have anything. That would have worked for him, too. But it was only a saying.

"You should start reading," his mom said when they got home.

"When pigs get wings," Drew muttered, but not loud enough for her to hear him.

That was another expression he'd learned from her. She used it when something he wanted absolutely wasn't going to happen.

He'd heard it recently when he'd asked if he could get a motorcycle.

Drew went up to his room and played a game. He had no plans to do any reading. It wouldn't be fair to call Drew a lying little weasel of a Weenie. It wouldn't be fair to weasels, that is. They deserved better.

At the end of the week, his mom took him to the library. He returned the three books he hadn't read and checked out three more he had no plans to read.

"Are you enjoying them?" Mrs. Folger asked.

"They're great," Drew said, which wasn't exactly a lie. He figured they could be great.

"That's part of the magic of summer reading," Mrs. Folger said.

Another week passed. And another. Eventually, summer passed. It was time for the summer-reading celebration party.

There was pizza, which was also fine with

Drew. His mom dropped him off, and told him he had to walk home. That wasn't fine, but it wasn't all that bad, either.

And then there was a book discussion, which totally wasn't fine with Drew. It was less than fine. It was terrible.

"I'd love for each of you to stand up and tell us a little bit about your favorite book you read this summer," Mrs. Folger said.

Drew waited to go last. Actually, he waited to go unnoticed. But he was not very good at avoiding attention. And, as he discovered when he was called on, he was even worse at faking things. It didn't help that he'd never even bothered to pay any attention to the titles of the books he'd checked out.

After an uncomfortable minute during which he tried to make up something about any of the books he'd lied about reading, he sighed and shut his mouth.

"You didn't read anything?" Mrs. Folger asked.

"I meant to," Drew said.

"Not even one book?" she asked.

"No," Drew said.

"One page?" she asked.

Drew shook his head. "Sorry."

She muttered something he couldn't quite hear and started handing out the prizes. In the end, when there was only one prize left, she offered it to Drew. It was a green umbrella with smiling orange goldfish on it. Nobody else had wanted it. Drew certainly didn't, either.

"Do you have anything better?" he asked. He was tempted to add, "Umbrellas are stupid," but he didn't think that would help.

She shook her head. "No. Real readers got all the other prizes."

Glad the whole thing was over, Drew slinked out of the library, walking right past the big *Summer Reading Is Magic!* poster.

"I wish I'd gotten a good prize," he said. "And I wish I didn't have to walk."

"Nay," someone said.

No. Not *nay*. It was *neigh*.

Drew found himself facing a horse. It stood right outside the library, as if waiting for him.

If wishes were horses, he thought. It looked like he wasn't going to have to walk home, after all. That was fine with Drew.

He got on the horse. "That's more like it," he said. "This is the kind of prize I deserve. I hope Mom lets me keep you."

As Drew spoke those words, he imagined what his mom would say when he asked her. He could almost hear her telling him, "When pigs get wings." And then, he heard a tremendous flapping sound, like huge birds were crossing the sky.

Even before he looked up, he knew what he was about to see.

Pigs.

They had wings.

They were flying right overhead.

Unfortunately, they were also going to the bathroom right over Drew.

"I wish I had that umbrella," Drew said, before he realized that this was a bad time to make wishes.

The wish brought more horses. And, since all of this was created by magic, those horses  had wings, too. They joined the pigs in flying above Drew. And in raining misery down on him.

Stinky and wet, Drew finally made it home. As much as he wanted to keep the horse, he managed not to speak his wish out loud.

Before Drew could slip down off the saddle, the horse bucked him off and ran away, which was exactly what it wished to do.

WHEEL OF ZOMBIES

I knew the zombies would come someday. Every kid knows that. I just didn't expect it to happen when I was so helpless.

I've always been prepared. I kept my hockey stick in my bedroom. Any zombie that tried to attack me there would get his head slap-shot into the next town.

My backpack was so crammed with books, it weighed about five tons. I could hold off a horde of stumbling brain munchers by grabbing the straps and whirling in a circle, like a guy warming up for the Olympic hammer throw.

I know this works, because I tried it once with my friends Dewey, Keith, and Megan. I sent all three of them flying.

My school was filled with all sorts of awesome anti-zombie equipment. There were fire extinguishers in every hall. We had some seriously dangerous liquids in the science lab. The wood shop was filled with sharp objects. The gym's storage closet had plenty of baseball bats.

Zombies at home or at school? No problem. I was ready.

Except, there I was, with Dewey, at the Baker County Firemen's Carnival. We're both big-time carnival Weenies. We love funnel cake, cotton candy, and sketchy sausages. And we love being in the middle of a crowd, with all the noise and action. But we don't agree at all on what the best part is. Dewey wanted to ride the Ferris wheel. I didn't. Ferris wheels aren't exciting. I wanted to play games and win a giant Pikachu.

The game I was trying sure looked easy. You had to knock three bottles off a table with just one ball to win. I've got a pretty good arm. I kept coming close. But I ran out of money, so I couldn't play any more games.

Dewey stood there the whole time, rooted for me like a true friend, and watched me lose, but he didn't play. Thanks to his lack of coordination, he hated games. But he had tons of ride tickets. He offered to treat me to a ride. I figured there was no reason not to go on the Ferris wheel even though it was so boring nobody else was riding it right now.

It was the open kind—just a seat with a back and sides, and a safety bar that didn't look very strong. I'm not scared of heights, so I figured there was nothing to worry about. Everything seemed fine, at first. The wheel was spinning pretty quickly, compared to some of the rides I'd been on, so that was good. I liked thrills. But it still wasn't all that exciting.

Each time we reached the top, I could see

the booth where I'd failed to win a prize. I was staring at it when the change happened. The thing about a carnival is that you don't notice screams. Not at first. Screams are part of the background noise. They had a couple rough rides, including a parachute drop and a Scrambler, so somebody was always screaming.

But screams are normally only one part of the noise at a carnival. When they become *all* of the noise, you notice.

"You hear that?" I asked Dewey as I scanned the ground below us.

"What?"

I pointed down at the screaming mob. Nearly everyone was running in the same direction. They were tearing toward the road that bordered the east side of the field. Which meant they were running away from the direction of the cemetery.

We reached the top again. I saw dozens of zombies staggering onto the fairgrounds.

"We have to get out of here," I said.

"Stop the ride!" Dewey shouted at the operator.

That's when I realized the operator had run off along with everyone else. I also realized the ride was speeding up. There was nobody to control it.

"We have to jump off!" Dewey said.

I watched how fast the ground sped past us at the bottom of our loop. "We'll get hurt. We're going too fast."

"It's our best chance," Dewey said.

Before we could argue about it, the zombies reached us. They stood on either side of the platform, trying to grab us each time we swooped past the bottom. I'd always thought it was ridiculous when people in horror movies were frozen by fear. But right now, my brain felt like it was spinning wildly inside my head, throwing off sparks and letting out screams. It had totally quit any tasks involving getting my body parts to move. I had to force myself to breathe.

"I have an idea," I said, after my brain decided to start working again. "Get ready to make a run for it when this thing stops."

I pulled off one of my sneakers, and took aim at the lever that controlled the ride. Right when we reached the bottom, I flung the sneaker as hard as I could.

"Missed!" Dewey said.

"But I was close," I said. I knew what had gone wrong. I wasn't throwing from a pitcher's mound, or from in front of a carnival game. I was throwing from a spinning Ferris wheel. I needed to take our motion into account. On the next pass, I threw my other sneaker.

"No!" I moaned.

I was just wide, on the other side of the lever this time. I'd overcompensated for the spin of the wheel. I turned to Dewey.

"Give me a shoe. I'm sure I can hit the lever this time."

"No way. I can't run good without them," he said.

"You can't run at all if they grab you and eat your brain."

"Good point." He sighed, removed a shoe, and handed it to me.

I took careful aim, and made a perfect shot. The shoe hit the lever with a hard smack.

"Great throw!" Dewey yelled.

"Thanks." I braced myself to leap from the seat and make a run for safety. But the wheel didn't slow down at all.

"Why didn't we stop?" he asked.

I was wondering the same thing. It took three more turns of the wheel, during which I almost got grabbed and pulled out of the car, before I saw what was wrong.

"I hit the side of the lever," I told Dewey. "But it has to be pushed from the front."

"This is hopeless," he said.

"Yeah . . . Wait!" A new idea hit me. "Give me the other shoe."

"Sure. I might as well die barefoot."

I took the shoe, waited for the right moment, and threw it so it bounced off the head of a zombie. I flinched as I saw his ear go flying. But I quickly turned my attention elsewhere.

The shoe shot toward the lever at the angle I needed, and hit the lever perfectly.

"Score!" I shouted as the lever moved the right way to slow us down.

I'd done it!

I hadn't expected the ride to stop so suddenly.

Dewey and I shot through the air, flying right over the safety bar.

We tumbled as we flew, and landed on our backs. I tried to get up, but I had the wind knocked out of me. Zombies shambled over and clustered around us in a circle.

"You okay?" I asked Dewey after I managed to sit up.

"Yeah. You?"

"Yeah."

"Why aren't they eating our brains?" he asked.

"Maybe they're afraid they'll starve," I said. I couldn't believe I just made a joke.

I stood up, and got ready to try to fight my way out.

The mob parted. The zombie I'd hit with the shoe came through the opening. I noticed he was missing an ear. I guess they wanted to let him have the first shot at me.

Then, I saw something else.

He was clutching a giant stuffed Pikachu.

He held it out to me and mouthed the words, "Nice throw. You win a prize."

"Uh, thanks," I said. "Sorry about the ear."

He shrugged as if it wasn't any big deal.

I looked around. Zombies were getting on rides and playing games.

"I guess they just want to enjoy themselves," I said.

Why not? They'd all been human until recently. Just because they'd become the living dead didn't mean they couldn't have fun.

"They do seem to be having a good time," Dewey said. "Back at the wheel, when they were reaching out, I think they were trying to save us."

I thought about the way they'd been waving their arms. "I'll bet you're right."

"Should we stick around?" Dewey asked.

"Maybe not." I noticed none of the zombies were at the food stalls. I guess they didn't crave funnel cake, cotton candy, or sketchy sausages. I hated to think what would happen if they got hungry. "We should probably get going."

I grabbed my sneakers and Dewey got his shoes. After we'd laced up, he pointed at the Ferris wheel. "Best ride ever."

I couldn't argue with that.

A FEW WORDS FROM A GRATEFUL AUTHOR

This is the part where I thank people who helped make this book possible, while you set the book down and run off to satisfy your sudden craving for a hot dog.

Without my publisher, Kathleen Doherty, and my editor, Susan Chang, this book would never have happened. Not many writers get to publish even one story collection, so I feel fortunate to be nurtured by the caring folks at Tor Books. The amazing Weenie art, first seen on the covers of nine Weenies story collections, and now seen both on the covers and scrambling across the pages of this first volume of Teeny Weenie Tales, comes from the wonderful mind of Bill Mayer. Author and bookseller Ellen Yeomans suggested I think about writing a collection for younger readers since my stories were popular with the older kids who came to her store. As you can see, I took her suggestion seriously.

On a personal level, my wife, Joelle, and my good friend Doug Baldwin, read and critique most of my work. My daughter, Alison, also gets called on when I need advice, suggestions, or someone to brainstorm with.

These stories were inspired by all sorts of things, in all sorts of ways. One of those inspirations deserves special mention. When I saw social-media posts from awesome young-adult librarian Andria Amaral about searching the beach for sharks' teeth, it gave me the idea for "Tooth Trouble."

That's all for now. I'd better get back to work. I have a lot more stories to write. There are still plenty of Weenies out there who deserve their moment of fame.

ABOUT THE AUTHOR

DAVID LUBAR credits his passion for short stories to his limited attention span and bad typing skills, though he has been known to sit still and peck at the keyboard long enough to write a novel or chapter book now and then, including *Hidden Talents* (an ALA Best Book for Young Adults) and *My Rotten Life*, which is currently under development for a cartoon series. He lives in Nazareth, Pennsylvania, with his amazing wife, and not too far from his amazing daughter. In his spare time, he takes naps on the couch.

ABOUT THE ILLUSTRATOR

BILL MAYER is absolutely amazing. Bill's crazy creatures, characters, and comic creations have been sought after for magazine covers, countless articles, and even stamps for the U.S. Postal Service. He has won almost every illustration award known to man and even some known to fish. Bill and his wife live in Decatur, Georgia. They have a son and three grandsons.